To kindred spirits, near and far —K.G.

To Clément, for his endless support during the creation of this book —G.G.

With undying gratitude to L.M. Montgomery for creating the classic story on which this book is based.

Text copyright © 2021 by Kallie George
Illustrations copyright © 2021 by Geneviève Godbout

Tundra Books, an imprint of Penguin Random House Canada Young Readers,
a division of Penguin Random House of Canada Limited

Library and Archives Canada Cataloguing in Publication

Title: Merry Christmas, Anne / written by Kallie George ; illustrated by Geneviève Godbout.
Names: George, K. (Kallie), 1983- author. | Godbout, Geneviève, illustrator.
Identifiers: Canadiana (print) 20200209876 | Canadiana (ebook) 20200209884
     ISBN 9780735267183 (hardcover) | ISBN 9780735267190 (EPUB)
Subjects: LCSH: Shirley, Anne (Fictitious character)—Juvenile fiction.
Classification: LCC PS8563.E6257 M47 2021 | DDC jC813/.6—dc23

Published simultaneously in the United States of America by Tundra Books of Northern New York, an imprint of Penguin Random House Canada Young Readers, a division of Penguin Random House of Canada Limited

Library of Congress Control Number: 2020934917

Acquired by Tara Walker
Edited by Peter Phillips
Designed by Jennifer Griffiths and Emma Dolan
The artwork in this book was rendered in pastels and colored pencils.
The text was set in a typeface based on handlettering by Geneviève Godbout.

Printed in China

www.penguinrandomhouse.ca

1   2   3   4   5   25   24   23   22   21

Penguin
Random House
tundra | TUNDRA BOOKS

Merry Christmas, Anne

INSPIRED BY ANNE OF GREEN GABLES

Written by KALLIE GEORGE

Illustrated by GENEVIÈVE GODBOUT

tundra

ADMIT ONE
AVONLEA HALL
7 PM 24 December

ADMIT ONE
AVONLEA HALL
7 PM 24 December

I'm so thankful for many things:
feathery frosts and silvery seas,
and wreaths as round as the moon.

But especially for this Christmas.
My first Green Gables Christmas.

To think . . . before, I didn't belong to
anyone or anywhere.

And now I'm *here*, in Avonlea,
where the trees gleam like pearls
and the fields are full of snowy dimples.

It makes me want to sing!

Tonight, though, I'm not singing.
I'm reciting poems at the
Christmas concert.

I tremble just thinking about it.
But it's a nice kind of tremble.
The kind that gives you a thrill.

And, *oh*, what a thrill!
A box tied with satin ribbons!

Why, Matthew, is that for *me*?

My first dress with *real* puffed sleeves!
Dear, shy Matthew, how did you manage?
And dear, sensible Marilla, how did you agree?

It is utterly exquisite.

I will wear it tonight for the concert.
I only hope I make both of you proud.

All morning, I practice my part.
I am a fairy and will wear a wreath of
wild roses in my hair.

At school, mean Josie Pye said
fairies don't have red hair.
I tried not to listen.

Later, Diana, my bosom friend,
comes by with *another* gift.

Beaded slippers from her Aunt Josephine!
The perfect match for my dress.
And perfect for a fairy.
It seems like a happy dream.

Oh, Winter, you make the world dream
as much as I do.

For lunch, we have a perfectly *dreamy* feast.
We eat Marilla's goose
and our neighbor Mrs. Lynde's pudding,
all laid out on frilly lace
and ferns I found that keep green,
from that certain deep hollow of the woods.

I *almost* forget the fluttery feeling in my stomach.
Almost.

Isn't Christmas a feast
    for the eyes as well?
Before the concert,
    we decorate the hall *divinely*.

Soon, the concert hall is aglow
with tissue-paper roses
and tiny candles that twinkle like they are dancing.

Diana says my hair looks almost auburn in the soft light.

At last, it's time.

Diana's solo is perfectly elegant.
Everyone is so splendid.
Even Gilbert Blythe,
who once called me Carrots.
And Josie Pye too.

I clap as hard as I can.

But then it's *my* turn.

I'm so nervous I almost faint, and I'm sure I can't begin.
But my new dress gives me courage.
I just *have* to live up to my puffed sleeves.

I think of Matthew and Marilla,
who haven't been to a concert in oh so long,
and perfectly prickly Aunt Josephine,
and Diana, my dearest friend,
and my many kindred spirits all around.

                                  And I know what to do.

The words come from ever so far away,
and I pour myself into them
and clasp my hands just so.

When I am done,
I see Matthew smile and Marilla nod.

And I feel like a star,
a lovely crystal one, all sparkling above the snow.

Snow crisps under sleighs,
and bells chime like fairy laughter
as everyone heads home,
where warm apple pie
and the cheer of the hearth wait.

On days when I am
awfully near despair,
and even I can't find words
to express how I feel . . .
I will remember
this Christmas.

And the very best
gift of all:
my kindred spirits,
who aren't as scarce
as I once thought.

I'm so very thankful
for you.

Merry Christmas,
dear kindred spirits.

Merry Christmas, Anne with an e.